## Dear Parent:
## Your child's love of reading starts here!

Every child learns to read in a different way and at his or her own speed. Some go back and forth between reading levels and read favorite books again and again. Others read through each level in order. You can help your young reader improve and become more confident by encouraging his or her own interests and abilities. From books your child reads with you to the first books he or she reads alone, there are I Can Read Books for every stage of reading:

### SHARED READING
Basic language, word repetition, and whimsical illustrations, ideal for sharing with your emergent reader

### BEGINNING READING
Short sentences, familiar words, and simple concepts for children eager to read on their own

### READING WITH HELP
Engaging stories, longer sentences, and language play for developing readers

### READING ALONE
Complex plots, challenging vocabulary, and high-interest topics for the independent reader

### ADVANCED READING
Short paragraphs, chapters, and exciting themes for the perfect bridge to chapter books

I Can Read Books have introduced children to the joy of reading since 1957. Featuring award-winning authors and illustrators and a fabulous cast of beloved characters, I Can Read Books set the standard for beginning readers.

A lifetime of discovery begins with the magical words "I Can Read!"

*Visit www.icanread.com for information*
*on enriching your child's reading experience.*

Sid the Science Kid: The Trouble with Germs
™ & © 2010 The Jim Henson Company. JIM HENSON'S mark & logo, SID THE SCIENCE KID mark & logo,
characters and elements are trademarks of The Jim Henson Company.
All Rights Reserved. Manufactured in China.
No part of this book may be used or reproduced in any manner whatsoever without written permission
except in the case of brief quotations embodied in critical articles and reviews. For information address
HarperCollins Children's Books, a division of HarperCollins Publishers, 10 East 53rd Street, New York, NY 10022.
www.icanread.com

Library of Congress catalog card number: 2009928956
ISBN 978-0-06-185258-9

Typography by Rick Farley
11 12 13 SCP 10 9 8 7 6 5 4
❖
First Edition

4745 4461 0/1 /12

Jim Henson's™
# SID
the Science
KID™

# The Trouble with Germs

by Jennifer Frantz

**HARPER**

*An Imprint of HarperCollinsPublishers*

"Sid!" said Dad.

"Breakfast is . . .

AH-CHOO!"

"Bless you, Dad!" said Sid.

"Bleh woo!" said Zeke.

"My dad is sick," said Sid.
"He and my mom say
that I have to wash my hands
if I don't want to catch Dad's cold."

"I want to know," said Sid.
"Why do I have to keep
washing my hands?"

Sid was super hungry.

"Wash your hands first,"
said Mom.

"Why?" said Sid.

"You don't want to
catch my cold germs,"
said Dad.

"I don't see any germs,"
said Sid.

"You're right," said Mom.
"Germs are too small for us
to see with our eyes."

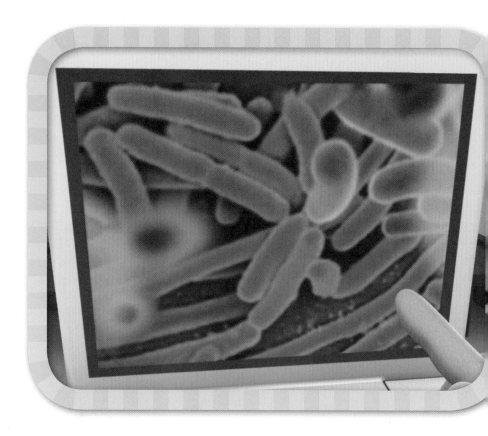

"Look," said Mom.

"These germs look bigger.
They are under a very, very
strong microscope."

"Cool!" said Sid.

"That one looks

like a robot."

At school, Sid met up
with his friends.
"Do you know what
germs are?" said Sid.

"Itty-bitty things

that make you sick,"

said May.

"Germs get on stuff.
And give you a cold
and stuff,"
said Gerald.

"Germs can make
you sneeze,"
said Gabriela.
"You guys know a lot
about germs," said Sid.

"Rug time!"

said Teacher Susie.

Sid and his friends

sat on the rug.

"Let's talk about germs!"

said Teacher Susie.

"We can't see germs,"
said Teacher Susie.
"But we can still pass
them around."

"Pretend that Gerald is sick,"
said Teacher Susie.
"He sneezes on his hands,
and gets germs on them."

"Then Gerald passes
germs to Sid.
And Sid passes
them to May,"
said Teacher Susie.

"It's like a big chain of germs!" said Sid.

"Always sneeze

into a tissue,"

said Teacher Susie.

"This helps stop germs

from spreading around.

Or you can sneeze

into your arm, like this."

Teacher Susie pretended to sneeze.

She covered her mouth

with her sleeve.

"Let's go to the
Super Fab Lab!"
said Teacher Susie.
"Time to learn why washing
your hands is so important."

"Pretend the dirt is germs,"

said Teacher Susie.

"Dip your hands in it."

"Cool," said Sid.

"I love dirt!"

"Now try wiping your hands off," said Teacher Susie.

"They are still dirty," said May.

"We need soap and water,"

said Gabriela.

"Right!" said Teacher Susie.

"It's the same with germs.

You need to wash up to get them off."

When Sid got home,

he was super hungry.

"Sid!" said Mom.

"It's snack time . . .

AH-CHOO!"

"Thanks," said Sid,
"but I think I will
wash my hands first!"

# LAUGHTERNOON
## a good time for some germ jokes

**What's the worst thing about being an octopus?**
*Washing your hands before dinner.*

**What do you get when you take a germ**
**. . . and another germ**
**. . . and another germ**
**. . . and another germ?**
*A cold! Ah-choo!*

**Knock, knock!**
*Who's there?*
**Ach!**
*Ach who?*
**Bless you!**